Postman Pat's Tractor Express

Story by **John Cunliffe** Pictures by **Celia Berridge**

*from the original Television designs by **Ivor Wood***

Hippo Books
Scholastic Book Services
London

Scholastic Book Services Inc
10 Earlham Street, London WC2H 9LN,

Scholastic Inc
730 Broadway, New York, NY 10003, USA

Scholastic Tab Publications Ltd,
123 Newkirk Road, Richmond Hill, Ontario
L4C 3G5 Canada

Ashton Scholastic, Box 579, Gosford,
New South Wales, Australia

Ashton Scholastic, 165 Marua Road,
Panmure, Auckland, New Zealand

First published in the UK by
André Deutsch Ltd 1983
Published in paperback by
Scholastic Book Services, Inc, 1984
Text copyright © 1983 John Cunliffe
Illustrations copyright © 1983
Celia Berridge and Ivor Wood
All rights reserved
Printed in Spain by Mateu Cromo, Madrid

Every summer, visitors came to Greendale, to walk in the hills and camp in the meadows.

"What lovely weather for people on holiday," said Pat, as he drove along the valley.

He called at the village post-office, to collect the day's post.

"Morning, Mrs. Goggins! Fine day!"

"Morning, Pat! Yes, and a busy one, too," said Mrs. Goggins. "Plenty of post for the visitors. The Jacksons are staying up at Birk Howe Cottage. There are some letters for them, so don't forget the extra call, will you, Pat? Oh yes, and there's a *registered* letter for those campers up at Southlands Farm. They'll have to sign for that, of course. I do hope you catch them in. *And* a parcel for Granny Dryden; I wonder what that can be?"

"It's a busy time, with all these people on holiday," said Pat. "I'll be glad when it's my holiday."

"Have a good day, Pat," said Mrs. Goggins.

"Cheerio!"

Pat was on his way.

He delivered his letters all along the valley.

All was quiet at Birk Howe Cottage. The Jacksons were away, and the only sound was the humming of flies and bees in the beautiful garden. But someone had left a gate open. And something unfortunate happened ...

Some sheep were nibbling the dry grasses outside the garden. Then, one of them found the open gate and wandered in. The grass in the garden was freshly watered and green. Lovely! The sheep began to crop the grass, trampling flowers down as it went. Two more sheep pushed through the gate, then another; then more and more, until they were all in, almost twenty of them!

They trampled, and nibbled, and pushed, and bleated joyously. They smashed down the flowers, ate all the lettuces, and broke a trellis. One put its foot through the glass in a cold-frame. What a mess they made in that lovely garden!

They were like a bunch of woolly hooligans. Then Peter Fogg came along, and shouted at them over the wall, but it was too late. He ran into the garden and began to chase them out. What a time he had! They hid behind hedges and dodged round trellises – they didn't want to go.

Then Pat arrived with the letters and came to help. He had chased sheep before. It took them a long time to get all the sheep out, and the garden was ruined.

"What a mess," said Peter. "It'll take the Jacksons the rest of their holiday to get this garden tidied up!"

"It isn't your fault," said Pat. "People should close gates properly in the country. I bet they'll not do that again."

"No, I don't think they will," said Peter. "Anyway, thanks for helping. Cheerio!"

Pat's next stop was at Granny Dryden's cottage.

She was so pleased to see her parcel, that she opened it there and then. It was her new catalogue from Manchester. It was full of pictures of things to buy.

"Is there anything you'd like to order?" she asked Pat.

"Let's have a look," said Pat, turning the pages.

He chose a digital watch, with a musical alarm.
"*That's* a funny watch," said Granny Dryden. "It doesn't look like a watch at all to me."

"Oh, it's a good one," said Pat. "It doesn't even need winding. It will help to keep me on time. Goodbye!"

Pat was on his way.

He had to go up the hill to Intake Farm with a letter for George Lancaster. George didn't often get letters, so he was very pleased to see this one.

"You'll be passing the campers, won't you?" said George. "Could you take them some eggs?"

"Yes, that's all right," said Pat. "I have a letter for them, so I'll have to stop there, anyway."

George went for the eggs.

"What beauties," said Pat. "I must take care not to drop them, specially as they're all in one basket . . . Cheerio!"

Pat was off again. He soon spotted the tents in the field, and stopped his van by the gate. But the tent's flaps were all zipped up and all was quiet.

Pat called,

"Hello! Anyone at home?"

But there was no answer.

"That's a nuisance – they must have gone off for a walk. Well, I can tuck the eggs under here. They'll be all right."

He put the basket of eggs in the shade, under the tent's fly-sheet.

"But what about this registered letter? I can't leave that, it looks too valuable, and they'll have to sign for it. I wonder if Miss Hubbard knows where they've gone?"

Miss Hubbard's cottage was just across the field. So Pat walked over, to see if she was at home. He was lucky – she had just cycled back from the village. Pat told her about the special letter; she knew where the campers were, all right.

"They've gone off to see the Gategill Waterfalls. They asked me the way this morning."

"Oh dear," said Pat, "that's at least six miles, and my van can't go along that old track."

"I'll borrow a tractor from the farm," said Miss Hubbard.

"Er . . . I can't drive a tractor," said Pat.

"Don't worry, I can," Miss Hubbard said; and off she went, for the tractor.

Pat wasn't sure that he wanted to ride on a tractor; but there was no other way. So he climbed on, and off they went. It was a very exciting ride . . . and a rough one in places. The track was all bends, and bumps, and holes.

There were loose places, where they went sliding and skidding. There were boggy places, where they squelched and splashed mud. They had to duck under low branches of trees, and Pat had to keep jumping down to open and close gates. He was glad when they arrived, but he was almost too sore and stiff to get off and take the letter to the campers.

But he struggled over the rocks to the waterfalls, where they were having a picnic. They were very surprised, and pleased, to get a letter there. When they had signed for it, Pat scrambled back to Miss Hubbard. And *then* they had to go all the way back again.

Pat was glad to see his van once more; but what was Jess gazing at, in the back? It was one of George Lancaster's hens – it had got in, somehow, and laid an egg.

"She'll have to stay there until to-morrow," said Pat, "but the egg will do nicely for my tea."

Pat was on his way home when he spotted a sheep stuck in a fence, so he stopped to let it out.

"I think that's my last job for to-day," he said; and off he went.

On his way home he spotted the Thompsons getting their hay in. "Ooooh, I heard about those sheep in Mr. Jackson's garden," said Alf. "Mr. Jackson was upset! Says he's going to get a new catch on that gate."

"A bit late," said Pat. "If only I'd been twenty minutes earlier, I expect I could have stopped them. Ah well – I'd better be off home now. See you tomorrow. Cheerio!"

"Goodbye, Pat!" they called. "See you to-morrow!"
They were answered by a clucking sound, from the back of Pat's van.